PUFFI

The Pocket Elephant

Other titles in the First Young Puffin series

The Pocket Elephant

Catherine Sefton

Illustrated by
Andy Ellis

PUFFIN BOOKS

PUFFIN BOOKS

Published by the Penguin Group
Penguin Books Ltd, 27 Wrights Lane, London W8 5TZ, England
Penguin Books USA Inc., 375 Hudson Street, New York, New York 10014, USA
Penguin Books Australia Ltd, Ringwood, Victoria, Australia
Penguin Books Canada Ltd, 10 Alcorn Avenue, Toronto, Ontario, Canada M4V 3B2
Penguin Books (NZ) Ltd, 182–190 Wairau Road, Auckland 10, New Zealand

Penguin Books Ltd, Registered Offices: Harmondsworth, Middlesex, England

First published by Hamish Hamilton Ltd 1995
Published in Puffin Books 1997
1 3 5 7 9 10 8 6 4 2

Text copyright © Catherine Sefton, 1995
Illustrations copyright © Andy Ellis, 1995
All rights reserved

The moral right of the author and illustrator has been asserted

Filmset in Plantin

Made and printed in Hong Kong by Imago Publishing Limited

Mary had an elephant that lived in her
cardigan pocket. The pocket was special. It
was an elephant pocket.

The pocket was lined with lettuce leaves
for the elephant to eat, and sometimes
Mary fed it bread and jam, which made the
pocket and the elephant sticky.

One day Mary took her elephant to
school.

"Good morning, Mary," said Miss
Wiley, her teacher.

"Good morning, Miss Wiley," said
Mary. "I've brought my elephant to
school."

"Why have you brought your elephant to school, Mary?" asked Miss Wiley.

"There are lots of books about elephants in school," said Mary. "I thought my elephant might like to read one."

"Right!" said Miss Wiley, and she got out an elephant book. Mary put the book in her elephant pocket for the elephant to read.

The elephant settled down to read it.

The more it read, the more amazed the elephant was.

The book wasn't about elephants in special pockets, it was about elephants in jungles, with lions and tigers to play with, and banana leaves to eat, as well as bananas!

Mary went to eat her school lunch, and she left her cardigan hanging on the back of her chair.

When she came back she got out the bread and jam from her lunchbox to feed the elephant BUT . . . the elephant had gone!

"Has anybody seen my elephant?" Mary asked anxiously. "It's a small sticky one."

Nobody had.

"ELEPHANT! ELEPHANT!" Mary shouted. Everybody else started shouting too, and running about the school looking for elephants.

There was a trail of small jammy
elephant footprints running down the hall
and over the mat and out the door.

"My elephant went that way!" Mary
cried, and everyone ran after it.

The elephant footprints stopped at the edge of the grass. By the time the elephant got there, the jam had all rubbed off.

Where was the elephant?

It was deep in the grass, like a big elephant in the jungle.

It didn't find any lions or tigers or
bananas, but it found some ants and a
centipede and a ladybird, and played with
them. The elephant ate a bit of daisy,
which it liked, and tried a bit of nettle
which it didn't like, because the nettle stung
its trunk.

Meanwhile all the children and Miss
Wiley and Mary were elephant-hunting,
but there was a lot of grass and not a lot of
elephant to look for, and they didn't find it.

They had to give up, and go back to
school. Mary cried, because she had lost her
elephant.

The elephant didn't know that. It was
having a great time playing with a mouse.

They played and they played and they
played.

"I really must go home now," said the
mouse.

The elephant went with it, but when they got to the mouse's house, the elephant couldn't get in. The mousehole was too small for the elephant.

And
it was getting dark.

And
it was getting cold.

And
it was getting late.

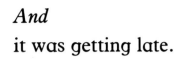

And . . . and . . . *AND* . . . there was a
CAT!

It was like the tiger in the elephant's book, but *bigger*, and it hadn't read the book, and didn't know about elephants. It thought it was chasing a funny kind of mouse.

The elephant ran, and so did the cat
and
WOOOOOOOOOOOOOOOOOOFFF!!!!!!
There was a dog!

It didn't know about elephants either, but it knew about cats. The dog chased the cat and the elephant and

SCCRAMMMMMM!
There was a man.

He chased the cat and the dog, and saved the elephant, just in time.

"What a small elephant!" he said, and he popped it in his pocket.

The man's pocket wasn't *meant* as a pocket for elephants. It had nuts and screws and bolts and a handkerchief in it, but the elephant didn't mind. It was much happier being back in a pocket than it had been running about in the jungle outside, which is what it thought the grass *was*, because it had never been in a real jungle.

Then

"E-l-e-p-h-a-n-t! E-l-e-p-h-a-n-t!"

The elephant heard a voice that it knew, and it started to wriggle and bounce in the pocket.

It was Mary and Miss Wiley, having a last after-school-look for the elephant!

"Pardon me, madam," said the man. "Have you lost an elephant?"

"Yes," said Miss Wiley.

"It was small and sort of sticky," Mary said.

"And frightened!" said the man, and he took the elephant out of his pocket.

Mary saw the elephant, and the elephant saw Mary, both at the same time.

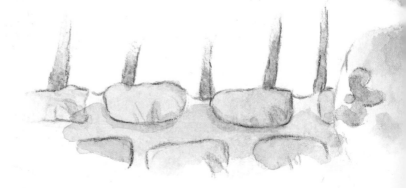

The elephant hopped off the man's hand and ran down Mary's arms and popped into its own special pocket. The elephant lay there, with its small elephant heart pounding and pounding!

Mary took the elephant home, and they both went to bed.

The elephant didn't *stay* in its pocket this time, as it did most nights. Mary took it into bed with her, because it was small, and still very frightened.

They both read the elephant's book, and Mary explained about jungles being great places for big elephants, but not-so-good for *small* elephants that live in pockets.

"But I'll be big some day, won't I?" the elephant said.

"Yes, you will," said Mary.

"Then I can live in the jungle!" said the elephant.

And they both went to sleep thinking about it.

Also available in First Young Puffin

BEAR'S BAD MOOD
John Prater

Bear is cross. His father wakes him up much too early, his favourite breakfast cereal has run out and his sisters hold a pillow-fight in his room. Even when his friends Dog, Fox and Mole arrive, Bear just doesn't feel like playing. Instead, he runs away – and a wonderful chase begins!

ERIC'S ELEPHANT ON HOLIDAY
John Gatehouse

When Eric and his family go on holiday to the seaside, Eric's elephant goes too. Everyone is surprised – and rather cross – to find a big white elephant on the beach. But the elephant soon amazes them with her jumbo tricks and makes it a very special holiday indeed!

RITA THE RESCUER
Hilda Offen

Rita Potter, the youngest of the Potter children, is a very special person. When a mystery parcel arrives at her house, Rita finds a Rescuer's outfit inside and races off to perform some very daring rescues.